A Home from Home

Written by Hawys Morgan
Illustrated by Monica Auriemma

Collins

1 The choice

Erin shifted uncomfortably from foot to foot. It felt like she'd been standing in line for hours. Her best friend Gwen squeezed her hand and gave Erin a small, reassuring smile. Erin squeezed back.

One by one, the children were selected by the grown-ups filing into the hall. The older, stronger girls and boys were picked off first. Next to be chosen were the neat and tidy children with ribbons in their hair and shiny polished shoes.

The flow of adults started to slow. Erin's stomach fluttered and turned. She glanced anxiously around the hall. There were only six children left. It was like the netball team all over again. What if nobody picked her? Would she go back to Swansea? Or would she be sent to a home for unwanted children?

She desperately smoothed down the creases in her skirt, pulled up her socks and put her best good-girl smile on her face.

Five, four, three children left.

Just two girls remaining, standing in the middle of the empty village hall.

Erin could feel her bottom lip starting to tremble. She squeezed Gwen's hand even more tightly.

"I mustn't cry! I mustn't cry!" she repeated to herself. She'd promised her mam that she would be brave.

Suddenly, the hall doors crashed open, and a woman accompanied by two young girls bustled into the room. "Am I too late? I'm always late! Where are all the poor dears?" She bustled over to Gwen. She didn't stop talking for a moment. "You must be shattered! What a long day you've had. I bet you're starving too! I've a delicious fruitcake at home, ready for you. I'm Mrs Richards, but you must call me Doris."

4

She took Gwen's hand and started to lead her away.

Erin felt like she couldn't breathe, as if she were being ripped in two. She felt tears prick her eyes and she tried to blink them away, but soon big salty drops were cascading down her cheeks as she cried out, "Please take me too!"

Doris stopped and turned back. She took Erin's hands in hers. "My dear, I wish I could. I've only room for one more child in my cottage. If I could take you, I would. But don't you worry, I saw Mrs Morton coming up the path. She'll take care of you, and she's got a lovely, fine house with a big garden. It's much nicer than my little cottage."

2 The big house

Mrs Morton was everything Doris was not.
She was a tall, thin woman with an impatient look
permanently painted on her face. She wore a smart
black dress and a hat over her black hair which
was pinned into neat curls.

She addressed the billeting officer. "I presume
all the evacuees have been taken by now?
You don't need any more hosts, do you?"

He replied, "Actually, there is one
child left."

It was the billeting officer's job to
find homes for city children here in
the Welsh hills. Since the war had started,
it was too dangerous for them to stay in
the cities.

Erin saw Mrs Morton's
shoulders drop. She felt the woman's
eyes survey her, noticing the tear-
stained cheeks, wrinkled socks and
the smudges of dirt on Erin's hands.
Erin wanted the hall floor to open
up and swallow her.

Mrs Morton sighed and
turned around. "Follow me,"
she said.

Erin's footsteps echoed on
the polished tiles of the entrance hall.
The silence of the house loomed
over her. Dozens of dark wooden doors
opened from the hallway.

One of the doors was ajar.
The windows were blacked out with
heavy black curtains. The furniture
was shrouded in large dust sheets.
In the gloom, they looked like an army
of giants.

"Since the war started, I've lost
all my help," said Mrs Morton.
"The butler, the maid, the chauffeur,
and my darling … my – " Mrs Morton
drifted off, then glanced sadly at an old
pair of wellington boots by the door.
She seemed lost in her memories.

"Your – ?" Erin prompted, curious.

Mrs Morton snapped back to
the present and continued briskly.
"They've all gone. Except Doris,
of course. Doris cooks for me once
a day and does a little cleaning.
I decided it was best to shut up most
of the house."

9

Mrs Morton led Erin into the dining room. One place was set at the long, polished table. "Sit," ordered Mrs Morton. "Eat."

Dutifully, Erin sat down and stared at the plate of chicken and salad. A wave of homesickness flooded over her. Why was she here in this strange house, with this strange woman? She wanted her mother, and the big old teapot that was always on the kitchen table, and the chatter of the street outside.

"Our soldiers on the front line would give anything to have a home-cooked meal. Eat, you ungrateful girl!" exclaimed Mrs Morton impatiently.

Erin tried to lift her hands to pick up her fork but the sadness and shock inside her made her limbs feel as heavy as lead.

"Don't you know how to use a knife and fork? Eat with your hands, if you must!"

Mrs Morton's rudeness jolted Erin into action. She managed to lift her fork and picked at the food on her plate. As she ate, she thought back to that morning. How different things had seemed then. It had all felt like a big adventure.

The whole school had arrived at the train station. Erin had been so excited. She had her small suitcase, a gas mask in a cardboard box around her neck, and a label with her name on it. Although she was a bit sad to say goodbye to her mother, she was excited too.

She'd never been on a train before. She'd never been to the countryside either. It felt like a holiday as she leant out of the train window, waving goodbye to her mam. She'd never stopped to think what being evacuated would actually be like.

3 Hide and seek

The next morning, Erin woke up in an unfamiliar bed. The starched white sheets felt stiff and unfriendly. She shivered, remembering where she was. She splashed her face with cold water from the ewer jug, pulled on her clothes and made her way downstairs.

"Erin!" Gwen almost knocked her over with a huge hug, as Erin walked into the kitchen.

"What are you doing here, Gwen? I'm so glad to see you!" Erin and Gwen had been best friends forever.

"I'm here with Doris." Doris smiled kindly from the stove.

Breakfast was delicious. A hot cup of tea, two boiled eggs and a slice of toast and butter each! Back in town, they only got one egg a week because of rationing, and neither girl had eaten real butter on toast since before the war started.

After breakfast, they decided to explore. "This house is perfect for hide and seek," said Gwen.

They spent a happy hour hiding all over the house, from the library with its hundreds of books, to the dusty attic filled with old pictures and crates of forgotten treasures.

It was Gwen's turn to hide, and Erin couldn't find her anywhere. Erin thought she heard a muffled noise from one of the bedrooms at the back of the house. She careered down the long corridor and burst into the room. "Found you!" she shouted.

A black figure jumped up from a rocking chair, and a copy of *The Jungle Book* fell to the floor with a bang. Erin screamed and tried to run from the room. She felt a cold hand close tightly around her wrist. She tried to wrestle free.

"Erin! What is all this hullabaloo?" The black figure was Mrs Morton.

"Wh … wh … what are you doing in here in the dark?" Erin stammered.

"I'll do as I like in my own house. You, on the other hand, will refrain from rampaging around the corridors. You are forbidden from ever entering this room. Do you understand?"

Erin nodded mutely and, as soon as her hand was released, she raced out of the room.

From that day, Erin and Gwen preferred to play outside.

4 Count your chickens

Erin loved spending time at Doris's cottage. It was
a ramshackle old place. A colourful jumble of things
filled every nook and cranny. Even though Gwen had to
share the big bed with Doris's two little girls, Erin would
have swapped places with her in a heartbeat. This was
a proper home: noisy, messy and fun.

In the morning, Erin and Gwen did chores for Doris.
Every day, they collected eggs from the chickens
and geese. It was usually a nice job, but sometimes
they'd come across Gregory Peck, the cockerel, strutting
around the hens, his beady eyes watching them.
When Gwen first arrived, she thought Gregory was
such a beautiful bird that she had tried to cuddle and
pet him. She quickly changed her mind when he came
flying towards her with his talons out!

"Look!" whispered Gwen. A stunning peacock butterfly fluttered past the girls. They put down the basket of eggs, pushed open the gate and ran after the butterfly into the lane. The heavy scent of honeysuckle in the hedgerows made Erin feel giddy. They followed the mesmerising butterfly over the fence and into the meadow.

The long grass came up to Erin's waist and tickled her legs. Bees droned sleepily around the wildflowers. The grimy, noisy streets of home seemed a million miles away.

Erin and Gwen started playing tag, the butterfly forgotten. Gwen waded through the grass after Erin, giggling and laughing. Erin ran on deeper into the meadow, shouting at Gwen, "You can't catch me!"

Suddenly, Gwen cried, "Erin! Watch out!"

Erin heard a deep snort, then an angry bellow. She turned to look in front of her. It was a bull.

Both girls screamed in unison. The bull was pawing at the ground, ready to charge. They half ran, half tumbled back through the meadow. The ground thundered as the bull pursued them. It was getting closer and closer. Gwen tripped and Erin pulled her back to her feet. They could almost touch the fence.

"We can do it!" roared Erin, and together they vaulted over the fence, just in time.

The bull glared at them through the bars of the fence, grunting angrily, but they were safe.

Erin and Gwen bent over, gulping in air.
Gwen laughed weakly. "That was a close shave."

Erin stood up straight and looked down the lane.
"Oh no. Look!"

A gaggle of geese and chickens were making their way busily down the lane towards them.

Gwen shook her head in disbelief. "We left the gate open!" All of Doris's geese and hens were loose in the lane and it was their fault.

Erin ran at the geese, trying to catch one, but it reared up angrily and pecked at her. Gwen tried to catch a chicken, but it darted this way and that. After ten minutes, red-faced and exhausted, the girls hadn't caught a single bird.

A tall, strong lad came strolling down the lane.
It was Aled Williams. He was from their hometown.
Erin sighed. As if the morning couldn't get any worse.
Aled was the school bully. He used to laugh at Erin's
glasses and throw stones at her on the way home
from school.

Aled stopped and took in the situation.
Then he picked up a large thin branch from the hedge.
Erin wanted to run away, but they couldn't leave Doris's
birds behind.

To her surprise, Aled turned to her
and said, "Let's get these birds back
to their coop, eh?" With that, he
started gently herding the birds back
up the lane, calling softly to them.
He used the stick to gently guide any
stragglers back into the group.

In two minutes, all the birds
were back in the garden with
the gate safely shut.

"Thank you, Aled! You're
a life saver," said Gwen.

Aled nodded curtly and walked
away chewing on a blade of grass.

"He's like a different boy,"
said Erin.

23

5 Letters

Erin arrived back at the big house, late for lunch again, with chicken feathers in her hair and knees streaked with green grass.

Mrs Morton sighed and dragged Erin to the kitchen. She scrubbed her hands and knees with a stiff brush, hard soap and cold water until they were red raw. "You'll stay in this afternoon, girl. You'll be quiet and you won't break anything," said Mrs Morton severely.

They ate their lunch in silence at the long table. Erin's heart ached for home. She missed her mam's laugh, her smell, her soft hair. She missed the scuffed kitchen table and chipped plates.

After clearing up lunch, Erin dutifully sat down and knitted some socks with Mrs Morton. They were big, grey socks for the soldiers fighting in the war. Erin glanced at the stiff figure sitting beside her. Even after several weeks here, she hardly knew anything about Mrs Morton. Who was she? What made her happy? Was she *ever* happy? Erin was too scared to find out. She bowed her head and concentrated on not dropping any stitches.

After knitting for an hour, Mrs Morton told Erin she could go to her room. Relieved, she climbed the long stairs. Her bedroom here was twice as big as her small box room back home, but at that moment she would have given anything for her narrow little bed, with its patchwork quilt and the soft rag rug on the floorboards.

Erin sat at the desk. She unfolded the last letter from home and smoothed out the creases in the paper. A tear silently crept down her cheek. She wanted to go home.

She picked up her pen, ready to write to her mother asking her to collect her. But she couldn't do it. She'd promised to be brave. She couldn't worry her mother and drag her away from her important war work at the shipyard.

So instead, she wrote a letter telling her mother how happy she was.

6 Gentle Rosie

In truth, Erin often *was* happy. The air was cleaner and the food was better here in the country. If only she could live here with her mother in a little cottage with a garden, then life would be perfect.

One warm afternoon in early autumn, the girls wandered up to the farm to see if they could pick some apples and pears for Farmer Jones. They found him in the meadow, stacking hay high on the cart.

"Fancy a ride on the cart?" asked Farmer Jones. The cart was hitched up to Rosie, his shire horse. The gentle giant neighed softly and flicked her thick fringe out of her big, brown eyes.

Gwen looked up at the hay towering above her. "I'm not very good at climbing," she said. Erin was already at the top, smiling encouragingly and holding out her hand to help Gwen.

After a few failed attempts, Gwen managed to scramble up. They whooped and clapped loudly, congratulating themselves on getting to the top of the haystack.

That was a mistake.

The clapping scared poor Rosie and she reared up on her huge hind legs before racing off at a gallop. Erin and Gwen yelped and grabbed on to the wobbling pile of hay as Rosie careered around the field, the cart swinging left and right behind her. The girls shrieked with laughter as they bounced up and down, holding on for dear life.

Gwen and Erin's laughter quickly turned to screams of fear. "Stop, Rosie! Stop!" Rosie thundered on. Farmer Jones hobbled after Rosie, but there was no way he could keep up. Rosie was making straight for the gate – the closed gate. A big shire horse would never be able to jump it, especially hitched up to a cart.

Erin shut her eyes tight, waiting to be catapulted from the cart.

Then she noticed they were slowing down. She opened one eye. Yes, the horse was definitely slowing.
She opened the other eye and peered down. Aled was standing in front of the gate, and he was murmuring quiet instructions to Rosie with his arms outstretched to her. Rosie slowed to a trot and approached Aled, who stroked her mane and whispered reassuringly to her.

"Thanks, Aled!" said Gwen.

"Yes, thank you," said Erin. "You've changed since we moved here."

"People can change," he replied. "Sometimes for better, sometimes for worse."

7 The dairy

Leaves floated gently down from the trees in the wood.
The children had conker battles in the overcrowded
school playground. A few months earlier, the village and
town children had been suspicious of each other, but
now they played together happily.

Erin avoided Mrs Morton as much as possible.
She would try to creep into the house without
being noticed. Mrs Morton was usually crouched over
her writing desk rereading old letters and writing
new ones. But letters rarely arrived for Mrs Morton.
Every day, she waited anxiously for the postman
to come. In these troubled times, the post could bring
both good and bad news. She seemed almost jealous of
the letters Erin received from her mother.

Erin spent more and more time at Doris's house. She helped as much as she could. She and Gwen weeded the vegetable patch, scrubbed the floor and washed the clothes. It was hard work, but Erin didn't mind.

The days grew shorter, and Erin often had to rush back to Mrs Morton's house before the blackout. Closing the blackout curtains was one of her jobs. It was an important job, too. They had to hide all lights from enemy bomber planes. Sometimes at night, Erin would lie in bed and hear the planes flying overhead. Were they headed for Swansea? She worried about her mother. What if a bomb dropped on their street?

Erin was walking back from school one day when she saw the most incredible sight. Farmer Jones was painting white stripes on his cows! "What are you doing, Mr Jones?" asked Erin giggling.

Farmer Jones looked at the cows and laughed too. "I suppose it must look rather odd! I need to paint them because of the blackout. All these cars and motorbikes are driving around without lights. There've been a few collisions between motors and livestock so I need my cows to be seen – I can't risk losing one of them."

He looked thoughtfully at Erin and said, "Doris says you're a hard worker. I don't suppose you could help out at the farm on Saturday mornings, could you?" He explained that most of his farm workers had gone to fight in the war. Aled was staying with him and loved working on the farm, but Farmer Jones wanted to let Aled sleep in one morning a week. "He's a good lad. He's great with the animals, but he needs some rest and time to study."

Erin happily agreed, but it was difficult to convince Mrs Morton. "You'll only bring more muck and dirt into the house," she warned. Eventually she gave in. She looked sadly out of the window and sighed. "I suppose we all have to do our bit."

On Saturday morning, Erin arrived bright and early at the farm. Farmer Jones was heading out to plough the fields. He pointed towards the cowshed and shouted, "Milk the cows, please, Erin!"

Erin called out, "I don't know how!" but Farmer Jones had already gone. She rolled up her sleeves. How hard could it be to milk a cow? Her confidence faltered as she surveyed the shed. The cows seemed much bigger in here than they did in the field. She couldn't give up now though; she didn't want Aled to find out she didn't know how to milk a cow.

She carefully approached one of the cows with a pail and a stool. She examined it closely. Where did the milk come from? She gave its tail a gentle tug. The cow mooed in annoyance and shifted in her stall. No, that wasn't it. Then Erin noticed the udders.

She sat on the stool and pulled gently on an udder. Nothing. She tried another one. Nothing. Feeling frustrated, she pulled harder. Milk shot from the udder straight into Erin's face. She gasped in shock and wiped her face clean. She tried again, and the milk shot off in the other direction this time. Erin looked in the pail – not a single drop had landed in there.

She tried again; this time a strong stream of milk hit the inside of the pail with a satisfying ring. Growing in confidence, Erin filled the pail and gave the cow a congratulatory tap on the rear. It mooed in surprise and kicked over the pail. Erin watched helplessly as the milk soaked into the straw.

She sighed but carried on, finally milking all the cows in the shed.

Farmer Jones was soon back from the fields. He showed Erin how to bottle the milk and churn some of it into butter. He gave her a pat of butter to take home. "You give that to Mrs Morton. I know she may seem strict, but she's a good woman under that hard surface."

8 Dragged from the depths

Winter came, and with it, there were new games for the town children to discover. They sledged down hills and had snowball fights. The snow was bright and clean, unlike the snow they remembered from the town, which quickly became dirty with soot and grime.

The river froze and the village children showed their new friends how to ice skate. The feeling of freedom as they glided across the ice made Erin's heart sing. Day after day, they returned to the river to skate with their friends.

Mrs Morton muttered with disapproval as Erin
tumbled through the door each day, leaving wet puddles
behind her, but she always had a fire blazing to warm
Erin and sometimes heated a mug of milk and honey
for her.

One glorious sunny day, Erin and Gwen went down
to the river as usual. They wanted to practise pirouettes.
They flew around the ice, faster and faster. The winter
sunshine warmed their cheeks.

A low creaking sound disturbed the perfect afternoon. The village children screamed and scrambled off the ice. Erin and Gwen were in the middle. Bemused, they came to a stop, not understanding what was going on. Then the ice collapsed underneath them, and they were plunged into the icy water.

Erin held on to Gwen as they sank. Neither girl knew how to swim. In a panic, Erin kicked her legs, and they broke through the surface, gasping for air before sinking into the freezing depths once more.

They resurfaced twice, feeling weaker and weaker
each time. Erin feared the third time would be their last.
Her clothes were sodden and they were dragging
her down. She wasn't strong enough to fight anymore.

A strong hand appeared from nowhere and grabbed
hold of Erin, hoisting her and Gwen out of the water.
Aled lay on the ice, spreading out his weight. A rope
was tied around his waist and the children on the bank
were holding on to it, in case more ice broke. Gingerly,
he dragged the girls along the ice and to the safety of
the bank.

9 An accident

Gwen and Erin were shivering violently. Their lips were blue and they could hardly walk. The other children wrapped them in scarves and coats. A boy offered his sledge. Aled pulled the girls to Doris's house.

Doris embraced the girls hard before pulling them into the cosy cottage. She heated up water in the kettle and slowly filled a tin bathtub that she placed before the fire. Slowly, the girls' frozen limbs thawed. Erin put on some of Gwen's spare dry clothing and a pair of old boots, while her own soaked things steamed on a drying rack by the fireplace.

The sky outside darkened – it would be night soon.

"You have to go back to Mrs Morton's," said Doris. "She'll be fretting about where you are."

"She doesn't care if I'm there or not. She hates me!" protested Erin.

"She doesn't hate you. She just has worries of her own," Doris insisted, and walked Erin back to the house, waving her off at the bottom of the path. "In you go now. It'll be blackout time soon so hurry up!"

Tired and tearful from the shock of her river adventure, Erin ran up the steps into the entrance hall. She stumbled in the borrowed boots which were too big for her. Erin tripped and fell, sliding fast along the smooth tiled floor before crashing into an elegant side table. A photo in a gleaming silver frame fell from the table, smashing onto the hard floor.

Mrs Morton ran into the hall and shouted,
"What have you done you clumsy, dreadful child!"
She picked up the broken photo frame, brushing away
broken glass. "This is my son, my brave boy. How could
you damage it! It's the only photo I have of him in
his uniform."

Erin stumbled to her feet, looking at the damaged
photo of a smart young soldier in Mrs Morton's hands.
"I'm sorry. It was an accident," she stammered.

Mrs Morton clutched the frame, her knuckles white.
She closed her eyes and hissed, "Get out of my sight!"

Erin ran out into the evening.

10 A new start

Mrs Morton knelt on the floor for a few minutes, gripping the photo frame. She looked out of the open door at the darkening skies. "Erin! Come back!" she cried. She ran to the door, but Erin was gone.

Mrs Morton grabbed her coat and ventured outside. She searched the shadows and called out until her voice was hoarse. The darkness thickened around her. Erin was nowhere to be seen.

Panic rose in Mrs Morton's chest. Erin was out there somewhere in the dark, alone and lost … just like her son. She thought of her poor William, fighting in France. She hadn't heard from him in months now. Where was he? Was anyone looking for him? Helping him?

She couldn't help William, but she could help Erin. Shame flooded over her as she thought of how cold she'd been to the girl. She should have been kinder, more patient. It hadn't been fair to take out her sorrow on Erin.

Mrs Morton raised the alarm in the village. Before long, a search party was looking for the little girl in the cold, dark night. Hours passed and worry grew.

Mrs Morton sobbed into Doris's shoulder. "We have to find her, Doris. Poor Erin. What have I done?"

There was a shout from the woods. Farmer Jones had found Erin wandering, lost and shivering, among the trees. Mrs Morton scooped Erin up in her arms and hugged her hard. Erin blinked in disbelief when she realised it was Mrs Morton. "Mrs Morton … is that you?"

Mrs Morton brushed away a tear and said, "You're all right now. I'm so sorry. So, so, sorry. I've been so unkind. That's all going to change."

Erin looked at the smooth, white hand held out to her and then up at Mrs Morton. The cold, hard mask was gone. In its place there was a reassuring smile. Mrs Morton said softly, "Let's go home and get you warm."

Erin took her hand and said, "All right, Mrs Morton."

Mrs Morton patted her hand gently and said, "Mary. Please, call me Mary."

Over a warm mug of cocoa, Mrs Morton told Erin about her son. She didn't have any other family in the world and hadn't received a letter from him since the spring. She was so worried about him.

"Seeing you race around the house, causing chaos, reminded me of William. He was just like you when he was little. It's been so painful being reminded of him every day and not knowing where he is. I bottled up all my fear and worry and it made me selfish and unkind when you needed me. I'm so sorry, Erin. Can you forgive me? Can we start again?"

Erin reached out her hand. "Of course we can, Mrs Morton ... sorry, I mean Mary!"

11 Home

When the war ended, Erin and Gwen went home to their families in Swansea, but they didn't forget all the friends they'd made in the countryside. Erin and Mary wrote to each other every week. Her last few months with Mary had been happy ones, and they'd grown close. During the day, they'd worked on a new vegetable patch in the garden together. In the evening, Mary had read William's old books to Erin by the fire.

The big house had become a home from home.

One sunny day, Erin and her mam took the train out of the city and headed to the hills. Mary met them at the station, and they walked back to the house together, stopping to say hello to old friends on the way.

"I've got a surprise for you," said Mary. They walked up the path and opened the front door. The house looked quite different now. The dust covers and blinds were gone. Sunlight flooded in. The heavy old furniture had been replaced with rows of neat desks and chairs.

Mary explained over tea. "It seemed silly, me rattling around in this big, old house when the village school is so crowded. So, I'm turning it into a new school." Erin and her mam thought it was a great idea. They poured over the plans with Mary, chatting excitedly. The house felt alive again.

Just then, there was a knock at the door. It was
the postman with a letter for Mary covered in stamps.
She eagerly read it, happy tears springing from her eyes.
"It's the most wonderful news. It's from William.
He's coming home!"

From a house to a home

homesick

nervous

scared

ashamed

54

sad

shocked

relieved

happy

Ideas for reading

Written by Gill Matthews
Primary Literacy Consultant

Reading objectives:
- ask questions to improve their understanding
- draw inferences such as inferring characters' feelings, thoughts and motives from their actions, and justify inferences with evidence
- explain and discuss their understanding of what they have read, including through formal presentations and debates, maintaining a focus on the topic and using notes where necessary

Spoken language objectives:
- articulate and justify answers, arguments and opinions
- use spoken language to develop understanding through speculating, hypothesising, imagining and exploring ideas
- participate in discussions, presentations, performances, role play, improvisations and debates

Curriculum links: History – a study of an aspect or theme in British history that extends pupils' chronological knowledge beyond 1066

Interest words: homesick, nervous, ashamed, shocked, relieved

Resources: IT

Build a context for reading
- Ask children to look at the front cover and discuss what they think is happening. Ask what the title means to them.
- Read the back-cover blurb. Explore what the children know about the Second World War and evacuation.
- Ask children how they think they would feel about being evacuated. Discuss the children's facial expressions on the front cover.

Understand and apply reading strategies
- Read pp2–5 aloud, using appropriate expression. Ask children why they think the chapter is called *The choice*. Discuss how Erin is feeling in this opening chapter and why. What do they think the children have in their suitcases?
- Ask children to read pp6–13. Ask how they think Erin is going to get on at Mrs Morton's. How would they describe Mrs Morton?